UNTAMED BUTTERFLIES

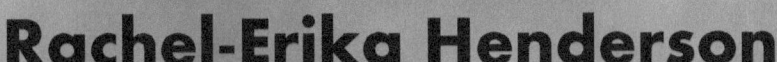

Rachel-Erika Henderson

Dedicated to James Douglas, Daisy Jo, David John and Ziggy Lachaise.

blurb

Douglas Donohue has lived in Pasadena (a city in California, northeast of downtown Los Angeles) all his life. Doug has always been blessed with an eye for creative art whether it is admiring or creating it himself. He is very handsome, tall and muscular with dark brown eyes, and wavy shoulder length hair. Doug is extremely well spoken, although incredibly shy, he is quite an extraordinary young man, his parents always said he had wisdom and knowledge far beyond his years. Doug tends to dress down to every occasion. Never far from his tan leather boots or his old buckled cowboy hat. Being a lover of art -also one of the few subjects he left school with a certificate in. He is drawn to expressing his creativity at every given moment.

At first glance Douglas's appearance is stereotypical of an uncouth illiterate drop out, but his personality is that of a spiritual being in search of the Dharma -his Dharma. He is friendly, kind, charismatic and unbeknown to him, his life is about to take him on one hell of a journey...

Douglas finds himself sat on a bridge railing watching the cascading waters thrash against the rocks beneath him. Something deep inside, a tiny ray of hope is giving him the strength he needs to reconsider his options. There was a downward spiral that lead him here to ponder his fate.

He once seemed so happy with free-spirited Joanne, a little naïve never the less but he had once loved this about her. Jo (as everyone called her) worked as a waitress at 'Aikendrum' a tiny cafe on the west side of town. Doug and Jo rented a small apartment not far from where Jo worked. Doug always introduced himself firstly as an artist, he was a very talented artist but like many, he was struggling to get his art noticed. John Steele was running an evening art class and as himself and Doug were good friends (being Doug's former High school teacher), John had convinced Doug it would be beneficial to broaden his art career by joining the class he was running.

Douglas hadn't ever really grasped the concept of John's erratic ways of teaching, however this time was different. The second week of class changed everything when 'Still life' became the following project. It was at this time Douglas met Erica. John's teachings quickly became much more interesting. Erica like Doug was a struggling artist and had volunteered herself as a still life model to get a bit of extra cash together and head up to San Francisco. This was the 60's, poets, artists and musicians were flocking to San Francisco's Haight Ashbury in a bid to express themselves freely (ultimately getting their work out there in hope of making it big). The time of revolution was in the air, war was over and the world was being unveiled in a different shade. Freedom, expression and creativity were in the air.

Erica first entered the classroom wearing a tight figure hugging crimson velvet dress. Her long black wavy hair fell just above her petite waist. Her bright red lipstick accentuating her beautiful pale ivory skin. Lifting her head to smile, revealing her piercing blue eyes, she was simply divine! 'Ok folks listen up' John announced to the class. 'This is Erica, she is going to be our life model for the next project'.

Douglas was taken in by Erica at first glance. When John announced Erica would be the subject for the next part of the course Douglas instantly felt something deep inside, like butterflies, untamed butterflies dancing about his body. Erica was not only beautiful she had a certain alluring aura about her. 'I want to see you all creating, use any brush, pencil or tool you so desire' John continued.

'A woman's body is one of the most beautiful and powerful things to behold'. 'If you feel earth child - create, a mother figure -create, love, sex, lust...' John paused. I want you to create not only what you see but what you feel' he finished. 'Well hello ya'all' Erica smiled giggling with a sweet southern accent. There were a few sniggers and a wolf whistle. 'OK, that's enough' John interrupted quickly.' A woman's body is sensual, but it also tells a tale of what she has overcome' he finished. 'You can get sorted in there my dear' John smiles to Erica pointing towards his office door.

Erica winks back before walking into his office carrying with her nothing but a colourful large leather patchwork bag. John is still busy talking but Doug can no longer hear a word, he stares at the door in a trance awaiting Erica's reappearance.

After what feels like an eternity Erica walk's back into the classroom, she is wearing a purple robe tied with a yellow satin cord. 'OK Erica just over there, on the seat by the window, there's a bit more light over there'. Erica complies simply walking over simply seating herself and dropping the robe to her feet, revealing every inch of her curvaceous naked body. Douglas's cheeks burn but he composes himself by clearing a space for his art tools, pencils, charcoal and paper, rolling out his bound leather art case. She doesn't seem phased at all, she sits silently still while the class produce their sketches.

Douglas draw's Erica's hands, they look soft and pure, angel like. He starts with her palms drawing them outstretched as if to reach for something.

After class most people head to 'Barry's bar' it's a dive, dark and dingy but open late. It's also frequented by some of the finest eccentric characters you will meet. Usually there's some kind of live musical gig on too.

Erica pulls her robe back up and on before going into John's office to get dressed. She appears again in the classroom grasping her patchwork bag trying aimlessly to squash her robe back in.

'So you coming to Barry's with us for a drink?' Douglas asks. 'I could absolutely murder a drink, but I got another sitting tonight' she winces. She pulls a journal from her bag and flicks a few pages. 'The Grange?' she reads 'you know where it is?' she quizzes Doug. 'Great, it's not too far from here' Doug smiles 'We got about three blocks' he winks.

'What are you a bodyguard?' Erica laugh's. At this time she thinks Doug is a bit forward, she doesn't know him and isn't too sure whether she is comfortable with a stranger escorting her. In the end she reasons with herself she doesn't know the way and this is cheaper than a cab. She accepts gracefully, they set off into the moonlit night. 'Hey you guy's coming to Barry's tonight?' ask's Bette one of Douglas's class mates. 'Nah we're groovy Bette, gonna show her the Grange' Douglas smiles. 'Lucky her' she laughs back.

They start their walk down a small cobbled brick lane.
'So what's your deal?' Doug asks Erica. 'What do ya
mean?' Erica replies. 'Like what's your deal, your
story? Everyone's got a story to tell' Doug smiles back.
'Well my story, let me see' Erica smiles looking
towards the sky. 'A couple mates and I just doing a
few random odd jobs in a bid to raise enough cash to
head over to 'San Fran' she finishes, before suddenly
pouring out her aspirations and dreams. She goes off
on a tangent. 'My dream is to go to San Francisco and
become part of it, you know to be part of this new
generation?' 'I can feel it in the air and I want to grasp
it with both hands' she continues. 'I want MY art to be
noticed and one day be hailed alongside the great's'. 'I
want to leave behind a legacy, my legacy, like my very
own Mona Lisa' she giggles. She continues describing
the world she envisions through her beautiful blue
eyes. Douglas would normally be bored by this type of
erratic conversation, but tonight he felt gripped. He
hardly utters a word, he just takes it all in, like that of
a spellbound audience.

'Well that's us here, this is the Grange' Doug stops
Erica as they reach a brightly lit Neon sign.
'Oh my' Erica stammers, embarrassed. 'I'm so sorry,
when you gotta sit still for that amount of time it's like
you kinda explode afterwards' she laugh's. 'How rude
of me, I didn't even ask your name?'. Douglas smiles
before giving her a sneaky peck on the cheek 'Doug' he
says winking and turning to walk on. Erica stands
under the sign for a couple minutes facing Doug as he
walks away she has a puzzled expression etched across
her face, but smiles before turning to head up the
stairs of the Grange.

Doug skips Barry's bar tonight heading straight home
with a brisk walk and a whistle. When he arrives Jo's
sat up with a joint waiting on him. 'Hey Dougie baby'
she welcomes him she is ever so slightly drunk. 'I've
been listening to some of Dave's L.P's and I found this
tune...' she trails off 'It's around here somewhere, on
one of these'.
'Oh my god Dougie you're gonna love it' she shrieks
stumbling about, then raking through the pile of L.P's
and knocking them to the ground. Douglas smiles 'Jo
baby, you're too high to find anything, let me help' he
says tidying up. He sorts through the pile. 'What song
Jo honey?'. 'It kinda go's do do da da du da...' 'Oh
Dougie just find us a tune' she yell's before dropping
the joint into the ashtray and slouching back against
the couch.

Doug searches a while before deciding on a bit of Ella Fitzgerald he lifts the needle to the turntable and places the record on before turning back to Jo who has passed out sleeping. He lifts the needle, switching off the player. He walks over to Jo, gently removes her shoes, before lifting her up to carry through to their bedroom. Doug lays her down, covering her with their old Tunisian quilt. He sit's down bedside her. Jo is ever so silently snoring but Doug is wide awake. His heart is racing, he feels so alive. He looks over to Jo, her silky fair straight blonde hair slightly covering her beautiful long eyelashes, she looks so peaceful. He loves Jo but sadly is no longer in love with her. They met at 16, and fate seemed to of paired them up. Doug found Jo childlike, and felt obliged to look after her.

Over the last 5 years it had gone from 'young lovers' to more of the love an older brother would have for his sister.
Douglas thought's turn to Erica. It was like a spark had been ignited. Although the whole situation seemed a little crazy, he'd just met Erica, besides what about Jo? Why was he even having thought's about Erica? On the confusion of this alone he falls asleep.

In the morning when he wakes Jo's already left for work, he can smell a freshly brewed pot of coffee, he get's up and walks into the kitchen. There's a note beside the coffee with a scribbled love heart, 'Try come home early Dougie baby, Let's just hang' Your Jo Jo x.

Doug sits down for a quick brew before heading to shower. He decides to leave the house early as today is a beautiful, the sun is shining, and he wants to embrace it. He walks to his favourite music shop 'Rudsy's rave cave' five blocks from the house. On his way Doug's mind is a whirlwind he keeps going over his relationship with Jo and this crazy spark he felt with Erica. Maybe it's lust, because she is absolutely beautiful, or maybe it's just a thrill because he's no longer in love with Jo? Never the less Doug is excited about tonight's class. He wanders down a little earlier and stops at Barry's for a pre-class beverage to whereby complete surprise he finds Erica sipping a scotch. 'Well hey there little lady' Doug surprise's her. 'Hey Doug, well if it isn't my very own chaperon' Erica smiles back. They share a smile before Doug perches on a stool next to her. 'I'll have whatever she's having' he smiles to the barman pointing towards her glass, 'and better get her another as well'.

Erica thanks Doug before they quickly lose themselves in deep conversation. This time Doug tells Erica about his love of art. How he wants to portray the world he see's.

It's not long before another couple from Doug's class Sheena and Matt appear. 'Hey Doug man, hey Erica' Matt smiles. 'Hey guys why don't you come join us?' Doug invites them over, the conversation quickly erupts with great debates and a lot of laughter all the while the drinks are swiftly flowing. They talk about films, debating whether 'The Birds' or 'Psycho' is Alfred Hitchcock's best creation. Girls voting Birds, boys Psycho. Before they all know it, it is time for class. The two couples head out into the early evening the fresh air makes them all feel a little giddy. They get to class with a mere few seconds to spare.

Doug, Sheena and Matt all take their seats and Erica heads through to get ready. Doug is a little half cut but Erica is as professional as ever. She reenters the room and once again lets her robe fall at her feet, positioning herself and the class begin to sketch.

Tonight Doug's focus is on Erica's eyes, he decides to use oil paint to bring out the prominent aqua coloured flecks inside her crystal blue eye's. After class everyone is once again heading to Barry's. 'So what you up to tonight?' Doug asks Erica 'you need to be walked anywhere?'. 'Well I could certainly do with some food after all that scotch then stillness' she smiles back. 'You fancy walking me back to mine for a bite to eat?' she winks.

'Of course ma lady' he replies in his finest put on English accent hooking his arm around hers. They set off into the night walking the four blocks back to Erica's. The night air is pleasant, there is a slight breeze, and with a brisk walk, it doesn't take long to get to her apartment. It has a small picket white fence surrounding it, dusted with a garden of colourful carnations. They walk up the steps to her front door, she unlocks it to reveal a quaint but modest apartment.

Small but perfectly furnished with a large bookshelf. There is also a lot of art everywhere. Doug walks in and over to a framed charcoal sketch of a legless soldier hung on the wall above above an old shelf. 'Wow' he smiles. 'Yeah?' Erica quizzes 'Some people don't really like that piece', 'I suppose art is supposed to be controversial, that man lost his limbs fighting for his country, he was the most beautiful caring soul' she finishes. 'You knew him?' Doug quizzes. 'Well how else could I draw him silly?'.

'You want a drink?' she questions.

'Got anything strong?' Douglas replies following her into the kitchen. 'Like more Scotch?' she asks lifting a bottle of Loch Dhu malt whisky from the top of the cupboard. 'Wow you are definitely a lady of complete class' he smiles back, before turning to gaze deep into her eyes.

He suddenly feels slightly aroused, like a boy in a sweet shop, wanting to taste every delight. Before he knows what's happening they are both in a tight embrace and he is sucking at Erica's top lip, she opens her mouth to let him in, they share a passionate kiss before he finds himself slowly tugging at her blouse. He pulls her in close, tight, sensually removing her garments. In amongst their tangle of clothing and kisses they both fall to the floor. He unclasps her bra strap revealing her beautiful swelling breasts. Erica widely opens her thigh's arching her back begging him to enter. He rubs his hand across her nylon pantys feeling her moistness. 'You are absolutely beautiful' he whispers.

He gently makes love to her there on her kitchen floor, passionately than he has ever knowingly made love before. Erica all the while gazes into Doug's dark brown eyes, she scoops his brown hair back from his shoulders revealing his muscular torso. There are no words or conversation just intimate kisses. They have both long forgotten about eating and retreat to Erica's bedroom. They continue making love between enriching conversation throughout the night, 4 AM arrive's and Doug regretfully decides he needs to go. He gazes into her beautiful blue eyes and kisses her forehead. Erica smiles back and rolls over to sleep.

Outside it is pitch black and cold. Doug doesn't know what he's gonna tell Jo, but right now he doesn't care, he has just made love to the most amazing woman he's ever encountered. There is some kind of kinetic energy he feels pulling him and Erica together.

When he arrives home Jo is sat up waiting on him, 'So where ya been Dougie?' she scowls. 'Oh man, sorry Jo honey I was at Dave's' Doug lies. Dave being a good friend to both of them -they all attended high school together. 'Had a late dinner after class and met Dave for a few drinks, I lost track of time' Doug finishes before heading through to the bedroom. Jo follows him laying down beside him, she attempts a cuddle. Doug half heartily cuddles her back just enough for Jo to get a slight hint of a faint floral scent. Doug falls into a deep slumber, but Jo is following her instincts. She creeps back through and makes a phone call. A sleepy voice answers 'Hello'. 'Hey Dave, sorry it's late babe, it's Jo, Dougie there?' she asks. 'Huh?, No not seen him Jo why? Everything OK?' 'Yeah fine Dave babe, sorry to disturb you' she replies. 'OK night then' he groans before hanging up.

Morning arrives and Doug awakens with a smile. He jumps up, wandering through to the kitchen. Jo has left for work already except this morning there's no pot of coffee nor love note in sight. Doug can still smell Erica's soft floral scent all over his skin. He brews a pot of coffee and sits to drink it, his mind racing even more so. All that is on his mind right now is Erica, he decides he must return to her sweet embrace.

When he arrives Erica is still sound asleep. He rouses her with a tender kiss. 'Hey Doug, you OK?' she yawns. It's in this moment Doug wants to pour his heart out to Erica and tell her of Jo, but he worries it will jeopardise any chance of a relationship so remains silent. 'Yeah of course baby, I need a breakfast date though?' he smiles. 'Well there are fresh eggs in the fridge, fancy some French toast?' Erica asks. She stands up cocooning herself in a blue tye dye blanket before wriggling over to the fridge. 'Hold up a minute sweetheart, I'll cook for you!' Doug exclaims.
'You go take a bath, relax baby' he insists. 'Well you don't have to ask me twice, if you're sure?'. 'Go Relax already!' he smiles back.

Erica obliges, and retreats to the bathroom. Doug searches through the cupboards to find all he needs to prepare breakfast.

After around 15 minutes Erica reenters with her hair tied up to the side, she is dressed in a blue floral silk kimono. She looks absolutely beautiful. Doug has finished creating a masterpiece of breakfast, not only is there 2 large plates of French toast but tomato halves cut into flowers and 2 tall glasses of freshly squeezed orange juice. 'Oh Doug wow' she smiles before sitting down, the two of them get stuck into breakfast. Erica talks again about

San Francisco how she can't wait to get there and show the world her art. Doug too, seriously wants to get his art noticed, both of them being creative talents share inspiring uplifting morning conversation.

Erica's idea of fine art is more controversial pieces, where Douglas's love of art is inspired more from the heart. Douglas loves the works of John Copley and Sandro Botticelli, whilst Erica is a dedicated fan of Andy Walhol, as well as Pablo Picasso, and Salvador Dali. Together they discuss artwork and the beauty of everyone else's perceptions.

'I can remember this one guy setting up a whole room of crushed aluminum cans for an art exhibition' Doug starts. 'Everyone was really into it, people were guessing what the meaning was behind his art, they were saying things like 'Wow man that's the strains of life', or 'It's about waste and destroying our earth and shit... so after the exhibition I went up to ask him what his art really was about' he laugh's. 'Yeah so what'd he say?' Erica questions. 'He said it was bullshit, his paintings never got any credibility and by setting up some household waste he was attending 'as an audience member' at his own art exhibition 'being the mentality of mankind'. Erica laughs 'Poor guy'. 'Not really' Doug smiles back 'In the end he was the one having the last laugh'.
They soon finish breakfast, Doug offers to wash the dishes while Erica picks up a floral tea towel to dry. 'Hey so today, wanna hang out, maybe go for a walk?' Doug asks.

'Of course Doug, I'd love to!' she smiles. Erica quickly goes to her room to get dressed as they decide to enjoy as much of the day as possible. It is a pleasant day, lovely and warm, being the first day of spring. They decide to visit the Memorial gardens spending their day wandering along beside plants and nature. They chat and philosophise about life goals, aspirations and dreams. The day passes quickly. Doug has quickly realised he is falling for Erica.

'Oh my' Erica looks up pointing at the tower clock, 'it's almost 5'o'clock' we got to get to class. They both embrace in grasp of entanglement and giggles, quickly hailing a cab to make it to class on time. They arrive on time to the minute.

Doug takes a seat and Erica who has left her belongings at home skips the robe, removes her clothing and positions herself. 'Pssst, hey Doug' Doug's class mate DJ whispers from behind him. 'Yeah, man?', 'What's your deal with her man?' he quizzes. 'It's nothing mate' Doug replies. 'With a body like that, you'd be crazy to not have anything going on' DJ sniggers back. 'You bet'cha' Doug smiles at DJ with a small hint of jealousy, he holds it together, finding himself all of a sudden questioning his feelings more so.

It's like Doug has some kind of love disease and Erica is his only medicine. Tonight every picture Doug etches' is Erica's face, highlighting her beautiful plump lips and sparkling blue eyes. This beautiful vision he wants to behold forever.

After class is over Doug and Erica decide to take a stroll through Glebe park. There are a few evening performers out and music fills the air. 'What a glorious night' Erica gushes dancing along only stopping to smell the roses.

'I just love these lil' old flowers' she smiles. Tonight
they talk about their families. Erica was born in Texas,
herself and her younger sister Emma had been raised
by her Grandmother Audrey. Sadly, at the time her
mother hadn't been able to cope with the 2 girls on
her own. They'd moved to Pasadena not long after
Erica turned 13 as her Grandmother thought John
Muir high had one of the best academic reputations.
Doug was an only child and money had been tight. His
parents Wendy and Gordon had always taught
Doug to follow his dreams and to listen to his heart.
Although different backgrounds their lives had been
very similar in choices.

Once again they end up back at Erica's. Doug decides
to come clean about Jo, but before he can Erica
interrupts.

'Doug honey listen, there is something I got to talk to
you about' she sighs 'I only got 2 days left here with
you'.

'What do you mean?' Doug asks. 'Well I have Thurs
night at your class, afterwards I got the Grange again,
Friday yours and Saturday well...' she trails off... 'We'
re finally heading to San Fran we have enough cash to
buy a car and get there to set up'.

Doug glances at the floor then looks at Erica deep into her eyes 'Do you feel it too?' he asks. 'It's like untamed butterflies?.

Erica's eyes begin to fill with tears she looks up, glancing deep into Doug's eyes. 'Make love to me Doug' she insists. Doug runs his hand up between Erica's thighs, He pulls her close, covering her neck in tender kisses all the way down to her buxom breasts. Erica holds Doug close, pulling his pants down below his backside. Doug's throbbing manhood is erect and brushes against her inner thigh. Doug tugs Erica's knickers to the side and pushes himself deep inside her.

She groans in pleasure through an enormous sense of well being. Throughout the night they share continuous climaxes and an intense explosive spiritual connection.

Doug announces he is coming with Erica to San Francisco. She tries to convince him otherwise but deep down it's all she wants too.

Tonight once again Jo is the farthermost thing from Doug's mind. Doug spends the night in a sweet floral embrace of pure intensity. 'Erica, I have never felt like this before, I love you' he whispers. Erica smiles back 'Y'all need to rest sleepyhead'.

They both fall asleep and awaken the following morning around 9 am. 'Morning my beautiful girl' Doug smiles. 'I got a few loose ends I gotta tie up today, but I'll catch ya later, in class'. 'Ok honey, you do what ya gotta do' Erica replies. Doug quickly gets dressed and heads back to finish things with Jo.

On his way home Doug's mind is racing with thoughts. He feels absolute certainty about something for the first time in years. When he finally arrives home Jo is waiting for him with a stern look. 'Dougie we gotta talk lover boy' she announces. 'I know Jo baby' Doug sit's down beside her. Jo takes his hand and before he has the chance to utter a word, 'Oh Dougie baby, I'm pregnant we're having a baby' she shrieks.

This bombshell instantly sends Doug's new world crashing down around him. 'We are?' is all he can muster up trying sheepishly to look delighted. How can he leave her now? She is going to be the mother of his child, she will need him now more than ever. Doug has suddenly acquired a newfound responsibility. He wants to feel joy, but instantly feels pain. It's like his heart is on fire and there is no way of putting out the flames.

'Dougie I've taken the day off' Jo smiles back. 'You want to skip class and catch a flick?'. 'Yeah course Jo babe, great idea' he utters blankly. 'Where ya been anyway Dougie baby? she asks 'Dave's again?' 'Yeah, Dave's' Doug replies. 'You two are like an old married couple' she winks back.
Doug goes to get showered, as the water is trickling down washing away every last bit of Erica's heavenly scent, he realises it's followed by an army of stinging tears. Doug collapses against the shower wall, and slumps to the floor in a heap. After what feels like hours he composes himself as much as he can to hide his puffy eye's from Jo.

He turns the shower off, climb's out grabbing a towel and using all his might to fight back any more tears. He gets dressed and heads back through to Jo who is waiting patiently.

They set off to the cinema in silence. 'You OK Dougie?', 'Yeah' he lies 'you've kinda stunned me Joanne'.

They arrive at the cinema where 'Zorba the Greek' is showing. They grab tickets and popcorn, sitting through the entire film. Doug does not take one bit of the film nor will he ever remember the title. Doug is sat beside his partner of 5 years, a woman whom he once was crazy about, she was now baring his child, but all he feels is pain. Like a strong force suffocating him, isolating him from his dreams.
After the film Jo suggests they should really tell her parents George and Mabel. George and Mabel are devout Catholics, George also being a retired strict army corporal. Doug and Jo's bohemian lifestyle has never been much up to either of their taste.

Doug is being lead around by Jo in some kind of a dazed trance. They hail a cab, heading over to George and Mabel's. When they arrive Jo's parents are sat on the porch.

George is engrossed in his newspaper whilst Mabel is sat with a glass of freshly squeezed lemonade. 'Hey mama bear, hey Papa' Jo smile's before kissing each of them on the cheek. 'Douglas and I kinda have an announcement'.

George pulls his Newspaper down peering up through his glasses like a headmaster glaring at an extremely bad pupil. 'Well... don't be mad OK, but we're having our very own baba' Jo exclaims!

Mabel senses George's rising temper and in fear of an explosion ushers them all quickly inside.

'That is the most ridiculous thing I've heard' George spit's. 'How on earth are you going to even support this child?' he shouts abruptly glaring at Doug.

Doug bends his head and shrugs 'I don't know sir, but I shall find a way of means'.

'You're not married' Mabel cries 'What will people think of us?'. 'Mama Stop' Jo begins to cry. 'If you both intend on keeping this child, I strongly advise you to both move away for a bit' George announces.

'You are going to need some kind of income to support a child and you cannot bring a child into this world before the congregation of marriage'. 'I can pull a few strings young man and get you a job in a silver mine up North' he finishes.

Doug's life as he knew it this morning is quickly caving in around him, like drowning in quick sand. All he wants to do is run towards Erica's loving arms.

He was a free spirit this morning ready to set off on an adventure of a lifetime with the woman he loves, now he is leaving this dream behind for the duty of fatherhood. He understands his previous resolution must be resigned, in order to repudiate responsibility. Doug brokenly accepts George's offer. George goes to make a few phone calls and upon returning informs Doug and Jo they will be heading off first thing in the morning to Calico silver mine. There they will have on-site accommodation, and there is plenty of work for Douglas. George and Mabel will drive them there personally.

'What about my job and Dougie's class and our wee home Papa?'

'You can forget about all that rubbish now Joanne, a child comes before any of that nonsense, I will sort out the remainder of the rent for your apartment' George scolds before his finishing quote 'Doug should be supporting you, he needs some good hard labour, a real mans work; .

Doug and Jo leave to go home and pack. 'Oh Dougie it'll be fine you'll see, at least we'll be together'. What kind of names are you thinking' she gushes, Doug's still in a trance 'Oh I dunno'. All he can think about is Erica and how to get to her one last time to at least say his goodbyes. They return home and spend the evening packing every belonging they can fit into 2 old leather bound cases. Jo decide's they should turn in for the night as tomorrow will be a long day, she falls asleep almost instantly but Doug is wide awake, his mind whirling, his heart pounding and his body aching.
He decides he has to see Erica one last time, throwing on an old coat he creeps out into the night. When he arrives at Erica's it's around 1 am, he bangs hard on her door. Erica opens the door looking as beautiful as ever, the moon light is shining down on her as she stands there before him in her blue kimono. Her dark hair is slightly covering the side of her face. 'Doug, Hey' she rubs her eyes 'where were you tonight?' she questions before seeing the stream of panic and fear etched across his face.

'Look Erica listen, God know's I love you' he starts to cry. 'Doug what's wrong?' she pleads. 'I gotta go away' he whimpers entering her house, he grasps her hands as tight as he can. 'You gotta go away?' 'With me still?' 'Still our plan Doug?' she quizzes him. 'No, oh God Erica please don't make this any harder' he begins to cry hysterically. 'You see, Jo's pregnant'. 'Wait who is Jo?' Erica demands. 'My girlfriend, Jo is my girlfriend', 'You have a fucking girlfriend?' she spits. 'Well no, I mean yes'.

'Well which one is it Doug because I'm assuming this Jo didn't just get pregnant by herself?' Erica screams', 'You have a fucking girlfriend?' 'What was I Doug, a fuck?'

'Get out you make me sick' Erica cries. 'Erica No, wait please listen, I love you' Doug shouts, 'I fucking love you, you're the one' he cries in pain.

'I'm the one? I'm the fucking one? Well what the fuck is your pregnant girlfriend Doug?' 'Just get the fuck out now you unimaginable asshole' she screams in amongst her tear's. All Doug can do is turn and walk away deflated and in pain. He has just hurt the woman he cares about more than anything else in the world. The walk home is long, cold and lonely.

When he arrives home Jo is still sound asleep. He looks at the two leather suitcases all packed up with his worldly possessions. Yesterday his case was going to be packed for dreams, today it seems as if it were packed for quite the opposite. Doug lays down on the bed beside Jo accepting this to be his fate now.

Morning arrives and Jo's up first thing making final touches. Doug wants to stay in bed forever but George and Mabel arrive early, ready to escort them off. They load their suitcases into the car and set off on their journey. It takes 2 long hours of silence to get there. They arrive at the small town of Calico. Calico is dark, dismal, colourless and empty. In fact it seems to be a town created for miners alone. There's an old church, a cemetery, a hotel, doctors surgery, post office, a few shops but really not much else. They drive up to a mine labelled the 'Silver King' mine, George parks the car before climbing out.

'Wait here' he demands before going to talk to one of the men on site.

After a few minutes he returns to the car. Doug and Jo are ordered to follow a man by the name of Peter Brent. Doug fetches the suitcases from out of the car. They follow Peter along with George and Mabel up a small hill to a caravan site. 'You are caravan 27, welcome to your new humble abode' Peter announces. He points over to a small orange and white caravan sat at the foot of a huge walnut tree. There's a communal kitchen to the left and bathrooms to the right he points out. 'I'll let you settle in son, see you back down at the mine 6 AM tomorrow morning' he says sternly before leaving. George, Mabel, Doug and Jo say their farewells, Jo hugs both her parents. There are tears from everyone except George, he turns to Douglas 'You do the rightful thing, you get enough money together to wed my daughter and support my Grandchild BEFORE returning' he demands like that of an army corporal. 'Yes sir' Doug replies brokenly.

Day 1 of work starts at the mine. Heavy equipment, shovels, pan, spades and 12 hours of back-breaking work. The only thing that gets Doug through his day is the vision he has etched in his mind, Erica.

Day 2 Doug makes friends with Wayne (a fellow miner) he and his fiancee Karen live in caravan 21, another 12 hour day of labour. Day 3 monotonous, repetitive back breaking work.

Doug receives one day off a week and that day is Sunday. Everyone on site is obliged to attend church first thing every Sunday morning. Doug seems to either be working or sleeping. Sunday afternoon is the only time he has to be creative. He is so exhausted he has barely muster any kind of conversation. It's like a wee tiny candle inside him is slowly burning out.

Day 24 Doug returns to the caravan to find Jo and Karen drinking. 'Jo do you think that's a good idea in your condition?' Doug asks.

'Her condition? 'oh that's righteous, leave her alone grumpy pants, your girl needs a bit of fun as you ain't giving her any!' Karen spits back.

Day 30 Doug is thankful he can still create the most beautiful art inside his mind. Every single picture he has painted inside his head for the last 30 days has been Erica. No one can take this from him.

By now 5 months have passed. Joanne had been at countless doctors appointments. Doug being so busy has not yet managed to go with her. He's lost so much weight and his once muscular torso is thin and waif like. She hadn't seemed to get much of a bump yet either. 'You sure our baby is Ok?' Doug asks, 'It's just you're so small Jo darling'. 'Fine, I'm fine, he's fine' she spits back. 'He?' Doug asks, 'Yes Dougie, It was going to be a surprise, we're having a wee boy' she gushes 'Just like you'. 'Why didn't you tell me?' Doug asks. 'It was going to be a surprise, I just didn't know when to tell you baby you've just been so busy' Jo reluctantly smiles.

'I'm so sorry Jo, I'm going to make more of an effort for my girl, I'll come with you to your next appointment I promise' he grabs Jo in a tight embrace as a tear runs down his cheek.

A week later Doug asks Jo about her next appointment, but she seems a bit blasé. 'I'll let you know Dougie'. Finally 2 more weeks pass. Doug comes home from work and Jo and Karen are surrounded by empty beer bottles. 'Jo you drunk?' he quizzes. 'Doug for God's sake give her a break man' Karen interrupts.

'Give her a break, seriously Karen?' Doug questions. 'Yeah man, why are you being such a drag?' 'A drag? You think any of this shit is good for the baby?' He yells thrusting an empty beer bottle under Karen's nose. 'What baby?' Karen stammers.

'What?' Doug asks 'How do you not know?' 'Jo is it true? You're pregnant? When?' Karen asks dumfounded. 'Look just get out please Karen' Doug yells. Karen looks over to Jo who's head is facing down towards the ground 'Jo?' she questions one last time before exiting the caravan. Doug grabs Jo by the arm 'Jo what has gotten in to you? Why didn't you tell Karen?'.

Jo looks up slowly at him, her eyes are red and her tears are coming in thick and fast.'Jo?' he demands. But she can't utter a word. 'Jo' he trails off 'Jo, our baby is OK right?' Suddenly Doug feels a realisation, a full force that hits him straight in the stomach like that of being winded. 'Jo?' 'Jo?' Jo looks at him. 'There is no baby is there?' Jo is sat silent for what feels like an eternity. 'No Doug, I was trying I mean I wanted to, you are just so tired and...' she trails off 'I'm so sorry, I need some more time Doug please' she begs. 'Need some more time?, For fucking what Jo?' 'What the fuck have you done?' Doug start's to cry sitting back burying his face in to his palms. 'I don't know' Jo cries 'But don't you dare act like the innocent fucking party, I knew' she spits back. 'You knew what Jo?'

'I fucking knew about the girl' she starts to scream back.
'Jo honey there's a big fucking difference there'. Doug yells at her. 'Oh my God, you are fucking psychotic'. Doug is trying to hold his anger, pain and hurt back for fear of doing something crazy.

'Please Doug we'll work it out' Jo cries. 'I fucking love you more than anything'.

'Doug listen please, I know I've messed up, but you don't know'. 'Don't know what?' Doug interrupts abruptly. 'The fear of losing you Doug, I love you so much' 'I am going crazy because I couldn't take the pain of ever losing you'. 'Do you know what Jo, I do understand' Doug says. They sit in silence again for what feels like hours. Jo is cowered in the corner crying like a child. Doug is sat with his head resting in his palms deep in thought, his mood is slowly changing. He looks over to Jo, he feels an intense amount of anger but also the pang of sympathy. His anger is quickly turning to pity. 'Jo' he stands up and walks over before kneeling down beside her. 'I understand how you feel, that's why I am always going to be part of your life OK'. 'I am going to make sure that I am part of your life forever Jo honey'.

'You are Dougie?, you mean you want to try for a baby?'.

'No Jo, no baby, but I intend to share some kind of relationship with you, we've been through too much' he grabs hold of her trembling hands.

'Come on girl, you know we've been through a lot'
'You have given me something to cherish forever'. 'I
have?' Jo winches, 'Yeah in some kind of mixed up
fucking mental crazy way, but Jo I love you and will
forever, just in a different way to the way you want.
'Jo you are like family, like my wee adopted sister and
I'm your big brother, I will always be there to look
after you OK?'.

'Oh Dougie' she wraps her arms around him pulling
him so tight he feels like he's about to burst. 'I think it'
s time we got outta here, I'm taking you back to your
Mum and Dads Jo' Doug insists, 'We're going to tell
them you lost the baby, and that is it, OK?' Doug
announces 'Understood?', Jo nods wiping her tears
aside.

They start packing up their stuff but into separate
cases this time. Doug goes to speak to his boss Peter.
Doug also tries to sort some kind of ride out of Calico,
he returns after about an hour. 'Wayne's giving me a
loan of his car Jo darling, Peter subbed me my
paycheck early we're leaving tonight' he announces.
Jo goes to say her goodbyes to Karen as she know's
she owes some kind of explanation. 'I'm so sorry
Karen, I just didn't know what to do, I guess I messed
up, I want you to know I never meant to hurt anyone'.

Karen takes pity upon her as well. 'You are crazy Jo but I'm still gonna miss ya more than words, besides who's gonna be my vent therapist now?' Karen smiles.

Karen and Wayne come to wave Jo and Doug off. Doug bundles their belongings into Wayne's beautiful sleek black Chevrolet Corvair before sharing a handshake and a hug. 'Look after her man' Wayne smiles (pointing at his car). They start their journey back to Pasadena, Jo falls asleep as soon as the hum of the motor kicks in. Doug's mind is racing faster than he is driving, he feels alive again with thoughts of Erica flooding back. It's been 6 months, he wonders if she's in San Francisco, if she's made it, if she's met someone else? He doesn't know how he's going to find her, but he simply HAS to. He envisions her face, her smile, her lips, her laugh. He visualises making love to her. The drive passes quickly, it's just gone early morning before he pulls up at Jo's parents and nudges her awake. The alcohol has worn off, Jo looks at Doug, open's her door and gets out of the car, steadying herself. Doug can see a broken little girl standing before him. He helps her to the front door with her suitcase. 'Remember what I said to say?' he asks, Jo nods. 'Alright Jo honey, you take care, I'll be back again real soon'. 'When?' she questions.

'I don't know Jo, but I'm giving you my word, I'm always going to be a part of your life OK?' he smiles kissing her cheek before walking back to the car. Jo stands for a few minutes watching Doug start the car, back up and drive off. She wipes the tears from her eyes and composes herself enough to go inside.

Doug has no idea where to go first but decides to call it a night, he needs a good rest. He finds himself parked up outside John Steele's house, climbing into the back seat he wraps an old blanket around himself and closes his eyes.

Morning comes too quickly, Doug wakes and goes to find John. John is already sat on the porch with a paint brush and a breakfast brandy. 'John' Doug calls walking up the porch stairs. 'Well son if it isn't my most prized pupil' he smiles back. 'Brandy's in the kitchen, you'd better pour yourself one' he finishes. 'Bit early isn't it John?' Doug quizzes before walking in and pouring himself a large one anyway. He walks back to the porch to join John. John is sat beside a canvas with a freshly painted outline of mountains.

'Real nice John' Doug smiles sitting down. 'How you getting on son?' John asks. 'I don't know John, I lost my way for a while but I'm gonna get it back!'. 'How far along is Joanne now?' John asks. 'What? how did you know?' Doug questions. 'The same week I lost my favourite pupil, my still life model was too upset to make her last day of class' John says. Doug stands up and starts to pace frantically. 'None of it was true John, Jo was never pregnant'. 'I gave up everything to support her and now, now I've lost Erica'. 'You were really smitten weren't you boyo?' John smiles back. 'She's been on my mind every day for the last 6 month's' Doug admits. 'Well I did hear from a little bird she's in San Francisco and that she's set up an art stall, but it could just be 'here-say' my friend'.
'That gives me some kind of hope John, even if it's just a glimmer, I just know I need to find her'.
'Look son why don't you stay here tonight?' 'You look like you could do with a decent sleep before you go anywhere', John suggests, Douglas obliges. He needs to gather his thoughts, to do that it pay's to be well rested.

John has a Moroccan stew boiling away on the stove top, the aroma smells divine, so after a few brandy's they decide to tuck into it for brunch. Afterwards they sit on the porch and share a few more. The conversation is Politics, mostly the difference between Eisenhower and John F Kennedy, being what they individually did for the country. It's a beautiful day the sun is shining and the birds are singing. Mid afternoon John decides his garden could do with a bit of maintenance so Doug offers his services. Doug mows the grass whilst John carefully prunes his prized rose bushes. When they are finished Doug decides he's earned a rest. He goes to lay down around 3.50 PM, but the last 6 months have suddenly caught up with him, he sleeps not only through the rest of the evening but right throughout the night. He rises early the next morning to the smell of bacon frying. He gets out of bed, following the scent down the corridor and into the kitchen. John is stood over a frying pan busy cooking breakfast.

'Ahhhhhh look he finally arises,' John teases'. 'How d' you sleep kid?' 'Yeah great thanks John'. John plates up some bacon and toast for the two of them. They venture out to sit on the porch with breakfast and coffee each. 'So I take it you're heading off to find her Doug?' John asks. 'Yeah John, I let her go once and my life deteriorated quickly', I just HAVE to find her'.

'Look son just remember life is a lot like surfing, sometimes your ride isn't the best, you get knocked down and thrashed about in the waves, but you got to get back up, and get back on that board because the next ride may be the most spectacular ride of your life' John grins.

'I suppose you never really know at that given time when you are actually experiencing one of the best times in your life, just the worst. I could be having one of those moments right now and I'll never know really until I look back' Doug replies. 'You got it kiddo' John winks. They finish breakfast in silence. 'Mind if I take a shower before I clear off John?' Doug asks. 'Of course Douglas, you could certainly do with changing your clothes' John laughs. Doug goes to wash before returning to announce it's time for him to leave.

Neither John nor Doug are really good at goodbyes so Johns 'OK catch ya later kid' is enough.

Doug sets off on his travels. He stops at a gas station on the outskirts of Pasadena to pick up a road map and a few refreshments for his travels, a can of cola, a baloney sandwich and a pack of gum.

He goes to pay the attendant before heading back to the car to study the map. It only takes him a short while before he is confident he knows the way, marking the route with a pen to be safe.

Doug begins his journey to San Francisco with the company of the car radio.

'The Beach boys -Good Vibrations' is playing. Doug's mind starts to go over the last few months, although right now he feels more alive than he has done in those months.

After a quick journey he finally arrives in San Francisco, not too sure really where to start.

At least he has the use of Wayne's car.

San Francisco is alive and buzzing, there are hippies, art, music, movements, an array of colour's everywhere. Doug finds a little Mexican style cafe called 'Arriba' and stops in for a drink and a slice of cake. He strikes up a conversation with a waitress called Melanie. Melanie is a bubbly brunette, a tad over friendly, but she seems to know a lot of folk and all the goings on. 'So what's the deal around here for an artist?' Doug asks. 'Well you're in the land of the hippie's, the musicians, the artists and the travelers too' she laughs.

'There's a big scene up the Russian hills, mostly weekends' Mel informs him. 'Hey you should come with us, we head up every Saturday, anyone who's everyone goes' she smiles.

'Hey listen, Mel man It's a long shot but you know a girl called Erica?' Doug asks. 'I don't know, maybe, I'm good at faces, names not so much' Melanie replies. Never the less Doug accepts Mel's invitation to head over with them on Saturday.

'Meet here at 'Arriba' Saturday morning around 10.30 OK?' Mel shouts out as Doug leaves. Doug smiles and nods before going to explore the city. He has the car to sleep in, so spends his days wandering. He visits gardens, museums, galleries as well as stopping for frequent refreshments in different bars. Anyone he briefly encounters he asks one question, the same question 'Do you know an artist named Erica?'. No one can shed any light on helping him find his girl.

John had mentioned to Doug he thought Erica had set up an art stall. Doug wanders round every inch of the city in hope he shall some how find her. That week passes quickly going from art stall, to gallery, to bar in hope that if she is here, he'll some how find her.

It's like he can sense Erica all around him, he just can't quite grasp her. Every evening Doug retreats back to the car with the radio for company. The big 610, KFRC keeps him entertained playing the likes of Janis Joplin, the Rolling Stones, Jefferson airplane and Bob Dylan, mostly.

Saturday finally arrives Doug heads downtown to pick up a newspaper before meeting Mel at the cafe. As he leaves the news agents and starts to get back into the car, he stops in his tracks, for a slight second. Doug thinks he can hear Erica's voice calling, his heart starts to race, he quickly turns to glance...

Nothing but the screeching of traffic. Doug shrugs, brushing it off before climbing back into the car. He turns on the radio and drives over to meet Mel at 'Arriba'. Mel and her boyfriend Tony are waiting patiently for Doug. 'Hey Doug you made it, this is Tony' Mel introduces them. Tony is the same height as Doug with dark brown matted hair, he is wearing black jeans, a bright yellow and red poncho and smoking a Gauloises. He reaches out to shake Doug's hand. 'Pleased to meet you man' he smiles 'You ready for some fun?' They leave to head over to Russian hills, Mel suggests they take the tram as a few of the customers have mentioned there's been some kind of accident in town and traffic is at a stand still. When they arrive Doug feels like he's found a piece of paradise. There is every colour of the rainbow in one small place, so many walks of life, like a giant haven of creativity.

Mel, Tony and Doug walk about soaking up the
atmosphere and the day. Mel introduces Doug to a
few people before they decide to seat themselves on
the grass verge beside the stage. Tony rolls a joint and
Mel flicks each of them an acid tab. The stage is huge
and performers are already lined up ready to put on a
show.
The three of them spend an afternoon enjoying
different sets throughout the day.
Next up is poetry readings, a scruffy guy introducing
himself as Andy takes the stage. 'I'll be reciting a few
of the poems from this years literacy awards' he
announces. He rambles off a few before he comes to
one poem.

'A beautiful world

an artist appears,

he opens his mind,

he blinds his fears,

He holds out his hand

she reaches to grasp,

He knows she's the one

he wants it to last

She looks at him

deep into his eyes

she feels it too

untamed butterflies'.

This poem instantly strikes a chord with Doug, It sounds so familiar.

It was Doug's life as he once knew it... with Erica. He used those exact words.

'Mel I gotta go speak to Andy' Doug announces. 'Geez Doug, you tripping?' 'He's on a fucking stage' she laughs.

'You gonna just walk up there and have a little chat?' Tony laughs. 'No man, but that poem, I know it, It feels like I know it, I think it's about me' Doug stammers.

Tony and Mel start rolling about in fits of laughter. 'You ARE fucking tripping Doug man'. 'I'm in a poem too man, the fucking mouse that ran up my cock' Tony laughs. 'No seriously man, I'm for real' Doug says 'I need to go speak to him'.

'Just wait man, Andy runs the show he's here all day so you can see him AFTERWARDS' Mel convinces Doug. He's not sure if it's the acid or the crazy feelings flooding back for Erica, perhaps a mixture of both. Strangely he feels Andy's poetry reciting is some way of fate providing a little hand in finding Erica.

Andy finishes his set and Doug hurries off to find him. 'Hey wait Andy, wait up man' he shouts running after Andy like a lion chasing it's prey. 'Yeah man, hey what's up?' Andy calls to Doug. Doug finally reaches Andy, trying desperately to catch his breath. 'The poem, Untamed butterflies' he stammers.
'The Author who's the author?' is all he manages to spit out.

Andy flicks through the compiled stack of poetry 'Um let me see... Erica... Stuart' he answers.

'Hey man, you know her?' Doug asks. 'Na man sorry, why you like it?' Andy questions.

'Well I think I might be in love with the author Doug announces.

'Any chance you know how to find her?'. 'Sorry man no, I'm just given a bunch of poems to recite, ain't no meet and greet in between' Andy shrugs. Doug pats Andy on the shoulders.

'Thanks anyway man' before turning to walk away leaving Andy a bit confused by the whole conversation.

He goes back to find Tony and Mel. 'Any luck mate?' Tony asks. 'A little' Doug smiles.'Hey where are you crashing tonight Doug?' Mel asks. 'Ole Chevrolet Corvair' Doug winks.

'In your car?' 'You have been sleeping in your car?' Mel questions. 'Fuck Dougie boy come crash at ours', It's our little squat!'. 'We got no hot running water' Mel says, before Tony interrupts 'But we got running water, we got candles and we got guitars, what more do you need?'.

'Well technically it's not my car' Doug smiles 'But I'd like to accept your offer as it beats sleeping curled up in any car'. 'Well technically it ain't our house either' Tony winks.

They take the tram back to 'Arriba' to pick up Doug's car before heading over to Mel and Tony's. The squat is run down but has remarkable character. There are last tattered remnants of lilac floral wallpaper on the walls, no carpet, but colourful persian rugs scattered about, as well as a few guitars, there are candles, colouful jars and paisley curtains hanging where each door once stood. Right now this is the perfect home for him.

As the weeks pass Doug ends up staying there with Mel and Tony, he finds a job setting up sculptures at events and concentrates on his artwork.
He still strives all the while to find Erica. At least now he has a last name if it was even his Erica that wrote the poem. I mean he felt a massive certainty the day he heard it but he was pretty wasted, did Erica even write poetry?

He manages to track down the company in charge of literacy awards but they are unable to give any personal information to the public.

Doug decides now he is settled he should really take the car back to Wayne. 'Hey Mel' Doug knocks on her and Tony's bedroom door 'Yeah come in'. Doug open's the door to walk in. Mel is sat on the floor reading an 'Atom ant' comic book. 'Look I'm going to head off for a couple days, you need anything before I go?' Doug asks.

'OOOh you find your girl?' Mel quizzes him. 'Not yet' he smiles back. 'So come, sit down' Mel pats the floor beside her. Doug walks over, standing directly above her. 'What's the deal with this girl man, she got a pussy that tastes like pot?. 'Ahhh Mel man' Doug blushes shaking his head. Before he has the chance to say anything else Mel stands up, puts her two fingers across his lips then removes them to unbutton her shirt. 'Mel what you doing?' Doug asks pulling away. 'Look Douglas honey, I'm telling you straight, you really need to let out some of your pent-up frustration it's not good for your zen'.

'I'm flattered Mel' Doug says moving aside 'But I wouldn't do that to Tony'. 'Oh relax Doug man' Mel laughs 'we're in an open relationship, besides it was Tony's idea' Mel insists. Doug is taken aback but slightly aroused by the whole situation. Mel runs her hand across the restrained member bulging inside his jeans, she unzips them slowly, unleashing his semi erect penis, stroking it like some kind of relic symbol. She pushes him back against the wall removing her panties and pushing herself up against him.

Doug feels the broad head of his cock at her opening. He caresses her inner thigh, moving up to unbutton her shirt, gently kissing her breasts. Mel mounts him using her hand to slip him inside her. Every thrust seems just a little deeper than the one before, and every thrust brings them closer to climax. Beads of sweat trickle down their backs.

Mel lets out a shriek of pleasure while Doug collapses back against the wall.

After a couple of minutes, they compose themselves.

'You don't need to find this Erica girl when you fuck like that!' Mel smiles through heavy breaths. Doug stares at her and they fall against the floor entangled. Just then Tony walks in and catches a glimpse of Doug's naked rare, his pants around his ankles, his manhood still inside his girl. Doug turns to meet Tony's gaze with a look of absolute panic. 'Relax man, it's cool… how was it?' he asks as cool as anything. He walks over to Doug and leans down to kiss Mel 'Alright babe?' he says. Doug cheeks flush beetroot red. 'Yeah pretty damn good' she winks with a grin. Tony playfully slaps Doug's behind.

'May need a go myself at some stage' he smiles before leaving the room. Doug feels extremely embarrassed and quickly pulls out of Mel.

'I'm gonna head for a shower and get some of my stuff together' he announces, collecting his clothes and quickly exiting the room.

Doug set's off on the journey back to Calico to drop the car back to Wayne. The car radio once again is his only company. The journey starts with The Kinks 'All day and all of the night' followed by The Doors 'Indian summer'. Every song that plays takes his mind to Erica. In between his thoughts and the music the drive passes extremely quickly. When Doug arrives Wayne is stood outside his caravan with a beer. He looks up with delight, Doug parks up and jumps out. 'Hey Doug mate, so good to see my wheels man, and you buddy, but really my car more!' Wayne laughs before grabbing Doug in a tight hug. 'So how are you guys?' Doug asks. 'Well we're finally getting out of this shit hole' Wayne smiles back. 'No way, that's great news man' Doug smile's. Karen has noticed Doug and comes to greet him too. 'Well hello stranger' she smiles wrapping her arms around him. 'How's Jo?' she asks. 'I've not heard' Doug replies. 'Me neither' Karen shakes her head 'I thought that girl was gonna be a friend for life'.

'So I'm up in San Francisco these days' Doug says. 'No way Doug man, bet it's awesome up there, come in and have a beer!' Wayne says inviting him in. 'We finally have enough money saved to put a deposit down on our dream home, well with a bit of help from Karen's parents' he announces as they clink bottles. 'Ahhhh man that is awesome' Doug smiles 'I really am so happy for you guys'. The conversation and beers are flowing and this continues long into the night. Doug ends up passing out on the couch staying overnight.

The next day a weary Wayne drives Doug to San Bernardino bus station. Doug purchases a ticket back to Pasadena, he feels he needs to 'check in' before heading back up across to San Francisco.

After an uncomfortable bus journey he arrives home to Pasadena. Ironically, one of the first people he bumps into is Dave. They get talking and Dave insists Doug has to come to a party in Longbeach later that evening, Doug accepts.

'So how's things going up there in San Francisco?, You joined a cult yet?' Dave jokes. 'Nah mate not yet anyway, Pretty good up there though, I share a pad with a pretty amazing girl and her fella' Doug smiles.

Dave and Doug spend the day hanging out in cafes, mostly catching up on lost conversation.

As early evening falls they drive down to the beach party. Doug wanders around talking to a few old mates before a familiar voice from the crowd shouts him. 'Hey Dougieeee' -it's Joanne, who comes running at him with open arms. 'She's like a moth to a flame that one' Dave winks moving aside. 'Hey Jo baby, how's my little lady?' he asks, trying to compose himself after her tight embrace. He has no animosity for her, just pity.

'Oh my God Dougie you are still so fucking sexy, we were so groovy together'. 'Take me now Dougieeee' she yells throwing herself at him. 'Jo baby you're drunk' Doug says removing her arms from around his neck. He brushes her off and moves away.

Doug tries to mingle a bit more before Jo starts throwing unwarranted drunken behaviour at him.

'I really fucking loved you Doug, how could you just fucking leave me?' she spits. 'Jo, give over' Doug finishes. He turns, lifts his feet and walks away.

He still holds on firmly to a glimmer of hope. Sometimes in life people follow the same path, other times you cross paths briefly, and then there are times the path you share comes to a crossroads and walking away is the only option. Doug had walked away from Jo in search of finding Erica's path once again and was still intent on finding his girl.

As the evening continues Doug and Dave join everyone around a crackling bonfire on the beach. There are a few guitars, a harmonica and an almighty engagement in many a song. Doug, Dave and a small group of others fall asleep on the beach beneath the stars. Doug has a great night although as morning arrives he can't wait to get back to San Francisco.

'Can't you stay Douglas man, it'll be like old times, It ain't the same around here without you' Dave pleads. 'Dave I have to find my girl' Doug insists before getting Dave to give him a lift to the bus station. He takes a bus back up to San Francisco.

When he finally arrives Mel and Tony are there to welcome him with open arms! 'Heyyyyy Doug' Mel smiles, Tony goes out to a handshake and as Doug does the same Tony pulls Doug in for a tight hug. 'Missed ya man' he smiles. It's late afternoon so they decide to head out and get a bite to eat. They go to 'Arriba'.

'Soooo Doug, we got some news for you' Mel pauses for a second before gushing 'I'm pregnant'.

'Is it...?' Doug starts 'Don't be silly man, you don't get pregnant that quickly' Tony laughs. 'All the dates add up, It's mine mate, I'm gonna be a Daddy!

'Well come here you guys and show me some Lovin'
Doug smiles scooping them both into a giant embrace.
'So what's your news? 'Mel quizzes, 'I'm still hell bent
on finding my girl' he smiles back.

Mel and Tony are both starting to think Doug sounds
like a broken record but they wince up a smile never
the less. They all order and enjoy lunch opting for
burgers and chocolate shakes before heading to 'Bar
109' (a new bar tucked down the next side street).
Doug and Tony share a few beers, Mel sticks to
lemonade. There's some kind of a jazz duet playing in
the corner, the atmosphere is buzzing and lively.

'So I've decided I seriously need to concentrate on my
art more' Doug announces 'I really need to embrace
my own inner creativity that's why I wanted to come
here in the first place'.
'As early evening arrives they head home. Doug goes
through his art folder finding his old drawings of
Erica. He digs out his pencils and paper and begins
etching away. His mind has kept her image clear and
all his emotions are pouring into his artwork. He
starts to draw her. There are butterflies dancing,
flames flickering and all the while in the middle of this
chaos Erica's face is portrayed smiling back at him.
Doug looks down at his artwork and smiles.

Tony walks in to Doug's room and gazes down at Doug's artwork, before lifting a few pieces to inspect. 'Man, Doug that is some fucking amazing shit right there' he insists. 'You really think?' Doug quizzes.

'I don't 'think, I know mate' 'You could be selling this stuff'.

Tony convinces him he needs to head down to market square and set up some kind of stall. Doug's hesitant at first but work on the sculptures is drying up literally. What he needs is some extra cash. Perhaps someone might even recognise the face in his art. Maybe just maybe this is what he needs to do to find his girl. He decides in the end it's actually a great idea and with a few phone calls he's in business as of this coming Saturday morning.

When Saturday finally arrives Doug is both nervous and excited.

'Relax Doug man, we're both coming with you' Mel smiles.

They drive across town to Market square. When they arrive the market manager 'Lucky' is there waiting to greet them. Lucky is older gentleman, slightly balding, round and exceptionally camp.

'Hey guy's just follow me' he shows the 3 of them around the market stopping for a short 'run down' before giving Doug a place to set up his art. 'We take a small cut, 20% per sale' Lucky advises Doug 'we do not charge you any rent on your stall'. Doug doesn't mind at all as he is happy to be here and happy to be embracing his creative side more so again. After a short briefing Lucky leaves them to set up. They get straight to work as well as enjoying the sunshine and the surrounding crowd. The markets are filled with musicians, artists, and so many different homemade trinkets and treasures. Before long Doug makes his first sale, a middle aged Spanish gentleman who is really taken in by Doug's art.

The gentleman is well dressed and extremely polite, although his English is broken and difficult to understand. He offers Doug $10 for one of his pieces. Doug jumps at the offer and the sale is made. Douglas gives his $8 cut straight to Mel and Tony who've been so good to him over the past while. This becomes a regular weekend stall for Doug, He spends the week creating and every weekend down at the market.

Doug is quickly starting to make enough money to get by comfortably. He soon makes friends with a wonderful little elderly lady at the next stall, Mrs Deijou. Mrs Deijou was born in Paris but had emigrated to America in her late teens. She was now in her 70's, very eccentric and shared with Doug many tales of her life adventures.
Doug confides in Mrs Deijou all about his love for Erica and his hope in finding her again. Douglas knows everyone else is getting a bit fed up, they think he's chasing after something that is long gone, not Mrs Deijou. 'Fate my dear has a funny old way of working itself out' she insists. She becomes his confidant mainly because she is the only one who never seems to tire from his endless stories of Erica.

As time passes at the stall Doug's artistic flair is being noticed and appreciated more and more often. Word of mouth is spreading, Doug's dream of making it in the art industry is starting to come true.

'Hey wow man your art IS as good as they say' smiles a customer. 'You really should be setting up your own exhibition' says another. After a little contemplating Doug decides this is the time to go for it, It's publicity for him but it's also throwing out a signal to Erica.

First, he needs a little help from his friends. 'Tony, Mel, I have a plan and I need you both to please help me' he pleads. 'Anything man' Tony reaches out to 'fist bump' Doug. 'Do you think you guy's could talk to Andy about letting me set up an exhibition at the Russian hills on Saturday?, I want to show case some of my work!'
'Well it's about time Douglas mate' Tony smiles. 'Let's get your work where it should be' Mel agree's. Tony makes a few calls to track down Andy, who's ironically just back from Venice and hasn't yet had time to line up many acts for the weekend. He gives most of Saturdays slot to Douglas. This doesn't give Doug much time but he see's it as fate giving him a push in the right direction.

'Man how crazy is it getting a slot just like that?' Doug beams to Mel and Tony. 'It's like it's meant to be' Tony agree's. 'Hey listen Doug man, I know you're still really digging your chick but people don't want to JUST see portraits of her OK?, 'They want to see an explosion of all your art creations'.

'Tony, I use my heart to create my art, she's imbedded in there' Doug insists. 'All I'm saying is we got you this gig man, don't mess it up for tales of a lost love' Tony interrupts abruptly. 'The Revolution is finally here, people want love, sex, identity, liberation, passion and freedom, you get me?' 'Yeah man I get it' Doug reply's.

Maybe Tony's got a point Doug reflects. Doug knows Tony and Mel are fed up of hearing about Erica, what if he starts to bore everyone else with his 'Erica' art. Doug regretfully decides to exclude every single portrait of Erica. He sifts through some of his work. Much of his art has been fueled from spending time at Market square. He paints colourful characters during any free time he has sat at the stall, including Mrs Deijou herself. He's heard most of her stories but he imagines the stories of everyone else in his paintings.

There's the small Indian boy playing cricket with his father in the park. He imagines this boys father has bought him to America for a better life firmly taking with him some of his Indian sporting culture.

The older thin, scruffy gentleman dressed in dusty moth eaten clothing who is sat on the park bench swigging from a brown paper bag. He looked like he hadn't known the pleasure of a shower or a comb in quite some time. At least he had a set of pearly whites and little lines at the corners giving his face the character of someone who used to smile often.

Doug pauses 'I have decided I am going to call my exhibition 'Unnamed happiness' Doug announces.

Tony and Mel get to work making up flyers for Doug's exhibition and pin them up around town. They also hand them out in various bars, clubs and pubs.

Time passes quickly and the day before the exhibition comes round. Tony, Mel, Doug, Andy and Andy's friend James head over to Russian hills and begin setting Doug's exhibition up for the following day. Doug will be showcasing a selection of 17 pieces of art. 'So as each piece of artwork is unveiled we'll give it a tinkle of a theme tune' Andy exclaims.

'First, we'll let the audience be captivated by your art then you can step forward and explain the meaning behind each piece, sound OK?' Andy asks.

'Sounds great mate' Doug smiles 'just need to conquer these nerves'.
Doug and James go through some L.P's trying to pair each theme with its appropriate painting.

For the Indian boy painting they choose
'Sun Sun Sun Didi' - Khubsoorat,
For Mrs Deijou Doug chooses Brigitte Bardot
'L'appareil à sous'.

Doug is feeling really anxious and queazy about
tomorrow and it is quite noticeable, 'You alright
Douglas mate?' Tony asks. 'Just nerves man' Doug
gulps. 'Wait until those curtains open tomorrow' Tony
winks. 'You'll be OK sugar plum' Mel winks.

'James will do the music and lighting all you have to
worry about is unveiling each piece and describing it,
the verbal description is just as important as the
visuals' Andy smiles.

'Ooh I can do the unveiling' Mel insists 'that way you
only have a brief description to worry about!' She
finishes.

Doug accept's Mel's offer. 'Thanks Mel that would be great' he smiles back at her. After they finish setting up they all head out for a few drinks and a bite to eat.

'Thanks guys for helping me do this' Doug raises a toast to his friends. 'It's a pleasure Andy smiles 'It's nice to have something a bit different and a pleasure to have an up-and-coming artist grace my stage'.

'Besides you can thank us all when you are really famous, I'd like a beach house in Bermuda' Andy jokes.

'Most artists get more gratitude after death' James pipes up. 'Well if the showcase is a flop, I'll kill him after the show and take the gratitude' Andy laughs back. They spend the rest of the afternoon laughing over mindless conversation.

'Guy's I am real excited about tomorrow but so fucking nervous about the whole audience thing' Doug admits. 'Nerves are good, you just have to learn how to channel them' Andy reasons with Doug.

They decide to call it a night and head home to get their heads down before tomorrow's big show.

Saturday morning arrives and Doug is so nervous he can't even manage breakfast. He forces himself to sip a small glass of milk so he doesn't have an empty stomach for the show.

'Come on guys' Mel shouts 'we'll be late'. Andy calls in quickly, asking Tony to collect James on his way. Andy is heading down early to tie up any loose ends before the show. They take Tony's car, Mel sit's in the back seat with Doug trying aimlessly to calm his nerves, holding his hand and going over each painting with him. They stop to collect James on their way. When they finally arrive at Russian hills, the place is mobbed. Doug starts to feel an anxiety attack coming on.

They park the car up behind the backstage entrance. 'Can you give us a few minutes?' Mel asks Tony and James.

'Yeah sure, get you in there babe' Tony smiles back.

Tony and James head inside. Mel hangs back with Doug. She finds an old brown paper bag squashed up in the back of the car and unwraps it getting Doug to breathe slowly into it.

She hopes this will help Doug compose himself, when that doesn't work she walks him about outside the car. 'Just breathe slowly and try to relax Doug' she whispers. They walk up to the back entrance doorway. 'Mel I can't do this' Doug panics, she grabs Doug and pushes him hard up against the wall.

She bends down towards him running her hands over his torso and around the back of his hips, unzipping his trousers, pulling out his manhood and licking the tip of his semi erect penis. Doug grab's her tight twisting her over him and up against the wall. He rubs the inside of her supple, naked thigh raising his hand across her leg and up her skirt, stopping at the hem of her panties. He pulls them down, pushing his two fingers deep inside her before using his throbbing hard cock to penetrate her. They are lost in an intimate moment of lust, Doug climaxes instantly.

Mel smiles and pulls her skirt back down before zipping Doug's trousers back up.

Did you get to...? Doug starts. 'No honey, that one was just for you, besides some chick in a wheelchair came round the corner and it kind of gave me stage fright' she smiles back.

'So listen Doug that's all the stage fright we have time for today, let's go give them a show OK honey?' Mel announces before taking Doug by the hand and leading him in to the building. They enter Doug nods to Andy, Tony and James positioning himself on the stage. Mel takes her place beside him. Andy picks up the microphone and walks through the curtain taking center stage. 'Hey everyone, welcome' he announces.

There is a loud roar from the audience and an encore of loud whistling. Doug starts to panic but Mel grabs his hand and holds on tight.

'Relax Dougie breathe' she insists.

'So you guys are joining us today for something a little different, but hey why not, this is the fucking 60's' Andy jeers the audience up. 'I am just seconds away from introducing you to Mr Douglas Donohue and his fabulous artistic visions'. 'Who know's this man could be the next Walhol and today he makes his debut on our very own stage' Andy continues. 'Enjoy the show folks, enjoy the art and be inspired'.

 The curtains are drawn back. Doug and Mel are fully aware of the sea of people that have come to see his show. Even Mel starts to feel nervous now. Andy hands the microphone to Doug. The main light shines brightly on himself and Mel. 'Hey everyone', 'Hey Doug' the audience cheers.

'This is Melanie and soon to be baby Mel' Doug smiles rubbing his hand across her belly, the audience gushes. Mel notices Doug is stammering a little with nerves, so she interrupts 'So Mr Douglas Donohue let's get the show on the road!' she shouts down into the microphone.

'White Rabbit- Jefferson Airplane starts playing and Mel unveils the first painting.

The first piece is a little girl with rosy cheeks sitting in a summer meadow holding an apple to her lips and grinning from ear to ear.

'I call this 'April sunshine' Doug announces before going into a short dialog of his painting and how he has used oil paints.

He decides it might be better to get the audience involved and to share perceptions. His nerves are starting to relax a bit more, mainly because the spotlight is shinning directly on him dazzling him, hindering the view of the large audience.

The next theme tune begins and Mel unveils the next piece 'Mrs Deijou'. 'Hey everyone what do you see in this painting?' Douglas questions. 'Geriatric?' someone in the audience shouts out, 'Age is beauty?' someone else jeers.

'This is Mrs Deijou, and that is what I have simply named this piece to honour her'. 'Mrs Deijou, is a good friend of mine' he continues 'She is a wee bit French and a wee bit American and a lot of an extraordinary lady'.

'The wrinkles across her skin are now so pronounced it is hard to tell what she must have looked like as a young woman'. 'They are deeply ingrained but they also tell a story of a woman who has traveled through more than seven decades to that one moment'. 'Each line on her face has been earned living the beautiful inspiring life she chose to lead'. The audience is captivated.

Mel continues unveiling each piece while Doug gives a brief description, as his show comes to an end Doug receives and almighty standing ovation. The curtains close and backstage they all breathe a sigh of relief.

'Well done man' Andy says with a 'high five'. 'Yeah nice one mate' James shakes Doug's hand. Mel and Tony both go in for a 'family hug' 'Dougie you did us so proud' Mel smiles. 'Doug man we need to get some prints made up and start flogging them around town you'd make a mint' Tony insists.

'Oh that's a good idea baby' Mel says. 'Come on honey let's go mingle' Mel takes Doug's hand and leads him out the side entrance. Doug is overwhelmed by the crowds of people, but Mel takes some of the pressure off by holding his hand tight, doing her best to answer questions from some of the awaiting audience. Doug loves Mel like a best friend most of the time, but then sometimes the sexual energy comes between them like an explosion, after that passes they're back to normal again.

They spend a couple of hours answering questions walking barefoot along the grass embracing the crowd and the glorious day. Afterwards they decide to head back inside to help the others get packed up.

'Look Douglas you can't say anything to Tony about our pre show encounter OK?' she quietly whispers.

'You see after I found out about the baby, well monogamy is our new kinda thing' she admits. 'Oh no, yes course Mel' Doug splutters 'I understand, 'But why did you?'

'I did it to help take your mind off your nerves Doug' she smiles back.

They both head back inside to where Tony, Andy and James are sat relaxing with a few beers James is holding an opened box of cigars, he tosses a cigar to Doug. 'That crowd is electric' Mel gushes.

'Yeah, we've been talking and wondered how you feel about auctioning off today's artwork next weekend?' Andy quizzes Doug. '90% directly to you and 10% to go back into maintenance and to keep the place ticking over?' Andy quizzes.

'Yeah course mate great idea' Doug smiles back.

Tony picks up a beer before shaking it and handing it to Doug, Doug shakes it a bit more before opening it and covering everyone in a light golden spray. 'Let's get rich!' he laughs. The next morning Doug feels emotionally exhausted.

He decides to skip his place at the market stall and lay in bed listening to one of his newly purchased L.P's (Joni Mitchell -Song to a seagull). Doug can hear someone banging on the front door, above the music. 'Mel, Tony can you get that?' he shouts. 'Jesus one fucking show Douglas and you're a fucking diva' Mel shouts back before going to open the front door. Doug can hear muffled voices so decides to go check it out, Mel is stood beside Andy.

'Douglas man' Andy says before pausing 'Your girl was there, Erica Stuart, she was at the show', he blurts out. "What man? Are you for real? How do you know?'.

Doug has so many questions he just can't get them out. 'She managed to track down my number, Andy announces.

'I asked her about that poem and you were right Doug, I actually thought you were tripping but you were right man'. 'Where is she? How can I find her?' Doug pleads. 'She just said to tell you she's so proud of you, and to follow your dreams', 'oh and to congratulate you and Mel' Andy finishes. 'Mel? 'No fucking way? She thinks we're together? Did you tell we weren't? Did she leave a number?' Doug asks. 'No man' 'She just said a few words, I asked her about the poem and then she quickly hung up'.

'Well we have to find your girl' Mel announces 'Doug wait, maybe she will come to the auction?' Doug holds on to hope that Erica may just reappear. The week passes very quickly, it's not long before auction day arrives.

Doug slowly scans every single face in the crowd but not one of them is Erica's. 13 out of his 17 paintings are purchased via an anonymous bidder by phone. Doug wonders if perhaps it could be Erica but his hopes are dashed when later in the day he receives a bank transfer from a Mrs Millicent Lowrage in Austria. The 13 sell at a grand total of $1300.00 and the other 4 sell to local businesses, in total he makes $1302.00 profit after his 10% deduction.

'So man what you gonna do with all your profit?' Tony asks. 'I gotta find my girl' Doug answers 'I just want to see if she's OK and let her know I ain't ever stopped loving her'.

Just like that Doug was back to his usual ways, back to searching for his lost love, back to his thoughts of Erica.

But no matter where he looked there were no traces nor leads to be followed. It's almost like she wasn't wanting to be found.

Doug decides to pay a visit to his old friend John Steele and manages to pick up a mint blue Ford Anglia for the ripe old price of a $550 cash. He drives back down to Pasadena to check in with his mentor and friend.
When he arrives John comes running out 'Check you out Douglas lad, you made it' John scoops him up into a hug. 'How d'you hear John?' Doug asks.

'Why you made it to the Pasadena national enquirer' John smiles back. 'Did you end up finding Erica?' he asks.

'No John' he frowns 'I have looked everywhere, but it's like she doesn't want to be found', 'Have you heard anything?' Doug asks John.

'I heard that she turned her back on art' John replies. 'Come inside and have a cuppa Doug'.

Doug and John go inside and John brews a fresh pot of coffee. 'Have you heard anything from Jo?' Doug asks John.

'Joanne has sadly gone down the heroin track my friend and she's having trouble finding her way back again' John replies.

'What about her parents?' Doug asks. 'Apparently they've disowned her, she is living with a bunch of addicts and from what I've heard there in no loyalty in amongst any of them' John finishes.

'Ahhhh shit man that's sad, do you think I should check in on her?'.

'It's your choice Doug, She might listen to you, but I'm pretty sure you didn't come back here to rescue Jo did you?'.

'John I came back because I am just as lost as I was before'.

'Art is my life, but I met Erica for a fleeting moment in time and in that moment she became my art, my life and then she was gone'. 'I have never stopped thinking about her John, I was hoping you may have been able to enlighten me in my bid of finding her once again' Doug pleads.

'Douglas all I heard is that she turned her back on art, but she also wanted to stay in San Francisco'. 'Her sister left here to go and stay with her'.

'The last thing I heard was that they were renting a small cottage on the outskirts of San Francisco'. 'It could even be hear'say my friend but that is all I've heard' John continues. 'Look Doug, I don't want to burst your bubble but by the sounds of it maybe, just maybe she doesn't want to be found?' he finishes.

'I understand John and I am kind of getting that same vibe, but there is a little shimmer of light inside that is still burning and telling me I HAVE to find her you know?', 'I understand completely son' John agrees.

They spend an enjoyable afternoon together before Doug decides to check in on Joanne.

John gives him an address he has for her. Doug drives up to an old rickety house.

There are a couple of kids playing with an old deflated basketball in the front scrubby patch of lawn. A small blonde haired girl who looks around 4 or 5 and a taller dark haired boy about 7 or 8.

Doug parks up before walking up the path towards the house. The children stop what they are doing and stare at Douglas.

'Hey kids do you know if Joanne lives here?' he asks. 'Yeah she's inside sleeping' says the little blonde girl. Doug walks up to the door, it's open. There is a rusty broken fly screen battering backwards and forth in the breeze. 'JOANNE? HELLO?' he calls out before entering the house.

The house is disgusting it has the stench of dirt, sweat and rancid fat cooked up a multitude of times. Doug follows the hallway down to the front room. There he finds a large burly tattooed man passed out in an armchair with a needle just hanging from his arm. He is face to face with the grim reality of the effects of substance abuse and addiction. Close by is Jo, she is passed out on the sofa wearing nothing but some old tattered underwear. She too has track marks all up her arms, she looks pale and haggard.

Doug glances about this hovel of a house before scooping her up and carrying her back to his car. ' Where you taking her? asks the little boy. 'We're going to get ice cream want to come? Doug asks. 'Yes please' the children both shout. 'Well get in then' Doug smiles back.

The little blonde girl jumps into the back seat squashing up beside Jo who Doug has placed down across the seats. The older boy jumps in the front beside Doug. 'Wow I've never been in an actual REAL motorcar before' the little boy exclaims. 'Really?' 'So what are your names?' Doug asks. 'I'm Melody' says the little girl 'M.E.L.O.D.Y' she spells out. 'I'm George' the boy replies proudly. 'Well I'm Doug and I'm honoured to meet you both' Doug smiles back.

He starts the car and heads in the direction of the beach.

'So where are your parents?' Doug asks.

'My Mum is in jail so Jo is looking after me for a bit' Melody replies. 'You're supposed to say she's at work Melody in case he's a cop' George turns to her and scolds. 'I ain't a cop' Doug laughs. 'My Mum died when she was having me and my Dad was sleeping inside' George admits. 'Was that your old man sleeping in the chair?' Doug asks. 'Yeah, that's him alright' 'he's always tired'.

They soon arrive at the beach and Doug parks up. 'Toot your horn pleaseee' Melody begs. Doug comply's numerous times and they all giggle. The three of them exit the car leaving Joanne passed out on the back seat and go to fetch some ice cream before heading back to the beach and finding a nice spot to sit. 'I'm gonna remember this forever' George smiles. 'We got to ride in a real car,' 'and we got ice cream' Melody interrupts. 'Well you two, I had better quickly check on Jo' Doug smiles. 'Stay here a minute would you?'.

He walks back up to the car where Jo is starting to come to. 'Hey Douglas, is that you?' she says dazedly.

'Jo listen to me honey, what on earth are you doing to yourself?' Doug asks. He offers his hand to help her out of the car. 'Nooooo it's too bright Dougie leave me in here. 'No Joanne you need to stop this' he grabs her forcefully by the arm and marches her over to where George and Melody are sitting.

Jo slumps over 'Hey kids' she sighs. 'She's always tired too' George announces pointing his finger at Jo. After about 10 minutes she comes round a little more. 'What on earth are you doing to yourself Jo?' Doug asks. 'I don't know Doug, I know I'm fucked up'. 'Do you know how to fix that Jo?, you are not only your problem, you are also your only solution!' Doug finishes.

Doug get's everyone back into his car and decides he is taking them all over to Jo's parents for some kind of intervention. He can't leave any of them like this. He pulls up and leaves everyone in the car before going to ring the doorbell.

Mabel answers the door but before she has time to utter a word George bursts out and grabs Doug by the throat.

'Stop it, 'George stop it' Mabel yells as she breaks them up, ushering them both quickly inside. 'Douglas what kind of monster not only impregnates my daughter but simply drops a woman when she has just lost a baby?' 'That baby being my grandchild?' 'You broke her, you broke my little girl' he shouts.

'Look George you are going to have to forgive me for that'. 'Right now I have your little girl and two beautiful children sat in my car'. 'You have 2 choices, either I take them back to the hovel in which I just found them and you lose your little girl forever' Doug continues 'or you let me bring them inside and you try to get her back'.

'It's not going to be easy, walking away is a guaranteed easier option, but if you truly love her' Douglas says before George interrupts abruptly 'Don't you dare put ultimatums on me!'. 'Who do you think you are? What gives you the right to speak to ME like that?'.

'Look George I didn't come here to argue, I just want to help Joanne'. George grabs Doug once again. 'Let him go now' Mabel shouts in a stern and frightening voice. 'Let him go George'. 'Douglas bring them in now, all of them' Mabel announces throwing a glare at George. George lets go of Doug. Doug exits, standing on the front porch he gives the guests in his car the nod to come in. Jo takes little George and Melody's hands slowly walking up the stairs, onto the porch and through the front door. 'Hi Mama, hi Papa' she muffles with her head hung towards the ground. Mabel grabs Joanne and holds her tight. 'My baby' Mabel howls, tears streaming down her cheeks. George steps forward.

'Who are these young children? he asks. 'This here is little George, Papa', 'He has a wonderful strong name, just the same as you' Jo says. 'He belongs to my friend Jeremy', 'This here is little Melody, rightful to her name she can sing the most beautiful melodies ever, can't you honey? Joanne smiles. She crouches down beside Melody who looks up at George and smiles nodding back. 'Melody belongs to my friend Sonia but I'm looking after her for now'. George looks down at the two children and then at Jo, it feels like yesterday Jo was only a small child, HIS small child. On this thought he can't help but grab Jo and pull her close. They both start to cry. Doug looks down at George and Melody, 'I'll remember this day forever too' he whispers.

'Kids I am going to go away for a little while now' Doug smiles. 'Are you going to jail?' Melody asks. 'Not quite darling, you'll see me again soon' I promise. Doug turns to leave, Mabel mouths out 'Thank you' to him from behind George's back.

Doug smiles and nods, he gets back into his car and begins the long drive back to San Francisco.

As his journey begins he thinks about all that has just happened. How he should've been there more for Jo. Although his dream of making it as an artist is coming true he feels a little defeated and lost within his own personal life. It's like he is constantly battling with his mind. Some days he feels like he is going crazy, some day's he feels numb. It is now approximately 1 year 6 months an 24 days since he last saw Erica. He remembers what Mrs Deijou had said 'Fate has a funny old way of working itself out'. Maybe he wasn't supposed to find Erica again. How was he supposed to live with that? He feels mentally exhausted.

It is a sunny afternoon around 4.30 PM when Doug stops off just before San Jose to stretch his legs and take in some of the view. He feels broken. Douglas finds himself sat on a bridge railing watching the cascading waters thrash against the rocks beneath him, something deep inside, a tiny ray of hope is giving him the strength he needs to reconsider his options. There was a downward spiral that lead him here to ponder his fate.

This would take it all away he thinks. But he reckons with himself it is a moment of madness and he pulls himself back in. He decides his only option is to give up on Erica. He needs to move on with his life. Maybe he should pack up and move to Mexico, his friend Georgie lives there, and she is always inviting him to stay. He has enough money now so what was stopping him? Finally after these thought's he composes himself and drives the rest of the way to San Francisco. It is late when he arrives but Mel and Tony are up waiting to greet him.

'Hey Douglas' Mel grabs him. 'You gotta come sit down OK? she say's looking panicked. 'What's going on Mel?' Doug asks. 'Just sit OK?' She takes his hand and they sit down together.

Tony comes out of the bathroom with a towel wrapped around himself. 'Hey Doug man' How was it?'. 'It was OK Tony' Doug says wondering why they have sat him down. 'Look we found your girl Douglas, well she kind of found you'.

'What? You guys know where she is? Doug asks. 'Look just listen honey, you just gotta listen' Mel replies.

'She was at the show, she came to see you backstage but she copped a bit of an eyeful and left.'

'What? Oh my god' Doug says, he looks at Tony, 'I'm sorry man'. 'Mel told me Doug man, but that shit doesn't matter right now' Tony says. 'Look Erica found you a long time before you found her.' 'What? Doug asks 'How'? 'Just listen Doug'. 'Do you remember the day we first met when we planned to meet up to go to the Russian hills that Saturday?

Mel continues, Doug nods. 'She found you that Saturday, she saw you go to get into your car, she tried to call out to you, but you never heard her Doug, so she ran to you'.

'You were getting in your car',

'Oh God Doug she wasn't looking at anything but you, she was struck down by a car'. 'Oh my God' Doug put's his head in his hands and begins to cry. 'The accident that day, the day we took the tram, Erica was the one involved in the accident' Tony finishes. 'She was in an induced coma for 5 months that's why you couldn't find her'. 'Sadly she lost both her legs Doug'.

'Oh my God' Doug cries out. 'She was the one in the wheelchair that you saw outside the backstage door wasn't she?'.

Suddenly everything is pieced together like a puzzle inside Doug's head. He remembered the day he was supposed to be going to meet Mel and Tony. He remembers after getting his newspaper heading back to the car. He recalls hearing what he thought was Erica's voice in his head'. Except it wasn't in his head. She had been calling him. 'So how can I find her?' Doug pleads 'Here is an address, Mel says handing him a piece of scrunched up paper. 'She doesn't know you have it, I managed to get it from a friend of a friend who is kinda hanging with Erica's sister Emma' Mel finishes. Doug decides to wait until the morning, what is one more day after all this time.

Although he barely sleeps a wink, when morning arrives he jumps straight in his car and drives to the outskirts of town. He pulls up at a modest but small house and gets out, running up the stairs and onto the porch. He tries the door, it's locked, he knocks loudly, no answer. He rings the door bell still to no avail. He tries to get round the side, but a high corrugated iron gate is in his path blocking him from entering. He reaches his hand up and manages to find a sliding bolt lock which he manages to open after a few minutes by reaching his hand through a tiny gap.

He pulls the gate back to reveal a huge garden full of roses, lily's, hydrangeas, and hyacinths. The aroma is beautiful and floral. He walks into the garden stopping briefly to smell the roses. He then turns and is met by the sight of the most beautiful thing he has seen in a very long time. There sat in a wheelchair covered with a red woolly tartan blanket is a vision he has been longing to see. 'Erica' Doug yells, 'Doug?' she replies. He runs to her, bending down to embrace her, pulling her close and gazing into her eyes, before stopping. He looks down and start's to pull back the tartan blanket.
'No Doug don't, please' she pleads trying to stop him. He rips the blanket back.

There before his eyes are just stumps where Erica's

Doug doesn't listen he runs his hands over her and looks deep into her eyes. 'Erica you are as beautiful as I remember'.

Tears are quickly filling her eyes. 'You know I once met this girl', Doug starts 'This wonderfully amazing, talented girl, a girl I have been looking for every day since' Doug continues. 'It's the only girl I have truly ever loved' Doug finishes as he begins to cry too. 'Oh Doug' Erica cries running her hand down his cheek to wipe away his tears. 'This girl' Doug continues 'she once drew a legless soldier and had insisted he had lost his limbs fighting for his country, and she'd said quote -he had a beautiful soul'. Doug smiles through the tears streaming down his cheeks.

'You remembered' Erica utter's in amongst her tears.

'What about your girl, your baby?'. 'There never was a baby, and Mel and her baby? Mel was never my girl'. 'Erica you have always been my girl, you have been on my mind every day since the first day we met' Doug smiles.

'I've just been figuring out how to get to you' Doug looks down at her. 'Doug look at me, how can you possibly love me now?' Erica cries. 'I live with my sister, who is now my carer, I need help to use the fucking toilet Doug, what kind of life is that for anyone?'.

'The only life I want is one with you in it, beside me' Doug whispers. Just like the soldier, it's your soul I'm in love with"all the other stuff is trivial, we'll work it out together'.

Doug gently lifts Erica up out of her wheelchair, her tartan blanket falls to the ground. He carries her inside. 'Where is your sister?' Doug asks.

'She's gone into town to collect some groceries' Erica replies sheepishly. 'Show me the way to your room', 'Doug I sleep on the couch, it's easier to get into my wheelchair by myself from there' Erica says with deflation in her voice. Doug carries Erica over to the couch, he lays her down.

'It is impossible to describe the overwhelming flood of emotions that a man feels when he sees the woman he has been waiting his whole life for, I can only try to show you how much I love you' Doug whispers. He starts slowly undressing her, she is hesitant, but he is gentle. She closes her eyes 'I haven't made love in the longest time' she whispers. Doug caresses her beautiful body all the while. He slowly moves his hands over where her legs once were, and up between her thighs. He tugs her knickers down and begins rubbing her slowly, she bites her lip as she feels his fingers gently stroke her. Doug releases himself from his trousers and slowly enters her, every inch of himself. He makes love to her slowly, gently, passionately. As pleasure erupts, they hold each other tight.

'Doug I love you, I have always loved you, 'the poem,

 I wrote and entered, it was for you' she continues. 'I had hoped if you ever made it here and perhaps found or heard that poem, you would know I loved you right back. I should have said it when I had the chance'.

'Erica, I never meant to hurt you and I promise I am going to spend every day of my life making it up to you, if you'll let me?' Doug smiles.

'Can you ever love me like this?' Erica questions.

'I will love you forever, for I know you're the one, I want it to last' Doug replies. Then she looks at him deep into his eyes she feels it too

Untamed butterflies...